T✡E
LOST
SISTER

BURT JAGOLINZER

Visit our website at www.StillwaterPress.com for more information.

First Stillwater River Publications Edition

ISBN-13: 978-1-950-33964-8

1 2 3 4 5 6 7 8 9 10

Written by Burt Jagolinzer
Cover by Emma St. Jean
Published by Stillwater River Publications, Pawtucket, RI, USA.

IN MEMORIAM

To the many, many millions of people whose lives were lost during the Second World War in Europe, Asia, and other important locations around the globe.

Also, to my recently departed significant other, Nancy Parenti who passed away after a battle with cancer on July 22, 2019. May she rest in peace.

PREFACE

When the Nazis came to his house in Poland during their invasion in 1939, they broke down the door, captured Ivan's father, and brought him outside where he was quickly shot dead.

Ivan's mother and sister, Anna, were taken away.

Ivan was beaten, processed, and eventually placed in a concentration camp for several years.

Ivan was told by a German guard that his mother was probably eliminated and that his sister, if pretty enough, would possibly be kept for use by the conquering officers... before eventually being killed as well.

This phase of Ivan's family story, as told in my book *Treated as a Jew*, is an imagined possibility that could have really occurred.

With this story, I create another adventure that takes place during the terrible times of the Second World War that had devastated Europe and the rest of the planet.

CHAPTER ONE

Anna and her mother were grabbed by two German soldiers and dragged out of their home.

When she looked back, she saw a soldier beating her brother.

She didn't want her mother to see the mistreatment to her son. "Please keep walking, Mom," she demanded in Polish.

Mom kept walking.

The soldiers quickly put them into a small captured Polish vehicle that took them to the first of several processing stations erected by the conquering Nazis.

They had already witnessed her father being pushed outside and shot. His body was left in the street covered with his jacket.

Mother and daughter expressed their doubt for the survival of brother Ivan.

Focus was now on their own future and it was not looking very encouraging.

When the vehicle finally stopped two female German soldiers helped pull them out of the vehicle. These two women were in uniform and carried guns at their waistline.

In perfect German, one of them shouted, "Take them to Herr Smidt."

Anna was nearly fifteen. She had finished two years of advanced schooling, learning both Spanish and German.

Her German was developed better than her Spanish. She had gone to school with two German girls who spoke German quite regularly.

Anna was able to put her newly acquired skill to good use.

She had come through adolescence with few problems and was at the entrance of womanhood when the war had begun. Anna was quite pretty, standing above five feet tall, with dirty blonde curly hair, hanging gently around her gifted face and nose.

Her outgoing personality completed her special character.

Anna reminded her Mom that she understood German quite well and to not worry.

Another female soldier appeared and the two of them pushed the captives to a truck at the far end of the parking lot that once served a now destroyed factory in this suburb of Belarus, Poland.

There, sitting on the tailgate of the large truck, was Herr Smidt.

In broken Polish, he addressed the two women who had been brought before him, "You must be prepared to tell your full name, religion and best skill. I will now allow you to have water before sending you further. No questions."

The same two female soldiers grabbed them once again, gave them each a swig of water, and pushed them in a different direction.

Behind the parking lot was a constructed tent. Entering, they observed a large counter desk with two male soldiers sitting behind the structure.

As they approached the desk, one of the male soldiers stood up and made a forceful statement, "You are to board a special train within the next hour to be sent to your next processing stop. We will make no exceptions."

They were immediately taken to a nearby train station where many other women and children were waiting, possibly for the same train.

Her mom suddenly cried out, "There is Cecile Borski, a member of our church!"

Cecile turned and whispered, "We have all been gathered for the same treatment, whatever that might turn out to be."

She stopped for a second and continued, "My husband Boris refused to join their military and was hung out our bedroom window, without clothes. He will certainly perish in the cold overnight."

Mom responded quickly, "You are not alone Cecile. We have similar tragedy in our family as well. We must wait and see what our future holds. Please God, we will need your help," she said as she looked up to the ceiling in the train station waiting room.

The train had arrived, and an officer blew his whistle demanding an orderly movement to the outside train entrance.

Female occupants were screaming from many of the boxcars in the front of the train.

CHAPTER TWO

They were pushed into a box car with a large group. The door was quickly closed and locked.

A whistle was heard, and the train began to move.

It was obvious that they were heading to a camp. But where?

Many in the car began to cry and shout as the turns on the tracks produced swaying in the box.

Some children were screaming at the top of their lungs. The overall conditions were poor and unacceptable to everyone.

The train continued. After several hours, the train began to slow down.

It had finally reached its destination.

The doors were opened and slid to one side.

Female Nazi guards awaited them. Some held rifles and pointed weapons at them.

In broken Polish, one guard began to speak, "Women with little children are to go to the right. Women alone must go to the left station."

At this point Anna was separated from her mother. With tears in both their eyes they waved good-bye. They were never to see each other again.

Her mother followed the line of women and children into a barn where their hair was immediately shaved off.

Next, they were ordered to take off their clothes.

When nude they were directed to a shower build-ing nearby.

The doors were locked, and poisonous gas was poured into the enclosed area, killing all the pris-oners.

Their bodies were carried out by other prisoners who would bring them to a nearby crematorium for disposal.

Anna was processed once again.

They noted her beauty and she was selected, with some others, to go to another tent where her head was shaved.

Because of her youth and beauty, she would not be killed at this point. She and the others awaited the next step.

They were told that they were to be transported into Germany. What that meant, they did not know.

CHAPTER THREE

There were some twenty of them, handpicked and ordered to board a large truck.

One woman in uniform, with pistol at her hip, jumped into the back of the truck with them.

Inside the truck were two buckets of fresh water and several loaves of brown bread. They were told by the guard to enjoy the sustenance. The trip to their next stop would be a long one.

Rambling through war torn Poland and finally crossing into Germany took most of the day.

The truck continued. The terrain changed immediately.

Germany was untouched at this time of the war.

They drove by columns of tanks, vehicles, and war-prepared soldiers moving in all directions. It was a show of military force that most of the world had not yet seen.

"How can the Allies stop them? They appear unstoppable. We are at their mercy," said one of the prisoners.

The female German soldier in the truck responded, "The rest of the world should throw down their arms and surrender."

It was near darkness when the truck finally stopped.

They were told to disembark from the truck and were escorted into a college sorority house which appeared to have been taken over by the military.

Female guards had been waiting for them.

Each girl received a blanket and towel. They were assigned rooms. The guards were everywhere.

Hot soup and cookies were offered in the main entry room.

They all moved quickly to consume the offered items. They were plenty hungry.

When they finished the offerings they were escorted to their rooms.

They were told that new prisoner uniforms were on each bed, and they were to shower and change into them.

The women were excited. It appeared that they were being treated exceptionally well. There must be a reason?

They were then told to have a good sleep, for tomorrow would be an important day for them.

.

CHAPTER FOUR

A large German military bus pulled up to the front of the sorority building.

The girls had just finished a small but meaningful breakfast of pancakes and meat, with terrible German coffee and bitter tea. Some type of butter was available, but one of the girls tried it and nearly screamed. It was awful.

They were instructed to leave the tables and form a line in front of the inside entrance.

Their names were read off from a clipboard. Finally, they were told to board the awaiting bus.

The bus took them around the college campus to a fraternity house that had also been taken over by the Nazi military.

A Nazi Officer boarded the bus and said aloud in broken Polish (and then in German) the following, "You are to become an engaging partner with important members of the Third Reich. You have been handpicked to treat these officers in your most feminine way. Your positive cooperation with them is imperative. Negatives are not acceptable and will be unfavorably dealt-with. They have been requested to treat you quite well. Food will be delivered to their rooms for you also. Please enjoy this special arrangement and you will be rewarded accordingly."

With that statement he began the assignments.

Anna Kanopsky was to be given to Dr. Hermann Berger, in room 212.

Hermann had grown up in nearby Dortmund. His neighbors and friends included several Jewish people.

His own family worked with several Jews.

They told him and his younger sister, Ida, of wonderful stories involving their close Jewish friends.

When the Nazi regime began blaming the Jews for their problems, he and his family couldn't believe it. They were worried for their friends and neighbors.

But there was little they could do. Soon, their neighbors were taken away by the military.

Hermann and his sister Ida became hopeful they could to do something to help.

When Hermann graduated from the local school, he was admitted into a credible medical school with the hope of becoming a doctor.

Upon his second year he was inducted, by force, into the Wehrmacht.

CHAPTER
FIVE

Hermann Berger never had the chance to become a formal registered doctor.

With only one full year of medical school, he didn't have the required study of the human body, nor did he have any surgical experience.

Yet the Nazis expected him to be a doctor, not caring about his credentials. They saw the need for eventual medical help in all their future aggressions.

Hermann and his sister Ida despised the workings of the Nazi regime.

They decided to do what they could to help save any of the people who were to be ruined by the terrible steps being instituted.

He was sent to this college, now under complete control of the military, where he was grouped with other medical professionals.

They received basic information and were presented with strict guidelines. They were also told of the penalties that could be imposed upon those who chose to go against the Fuhrer's requirements.

Hermann knew he had to do his job, but he would always look for ways to help individuals when opportunities arrived.

His sister Ida, who was now sixteen and wanted to be a nurse, volunteered at the campus hospital just outside the college campus in Dortmund.

She was given a job in the emergency area at the entrance to the facility. A room in the rear building was given to her, along with the other nurses and volunteers.

Ida and Hermann vowed to keep in touch, but she knew that Hermann would eventually be re-assigned to another location, possibly out of the country.

Hermann and his group had finished abbreviated training and their assignments were only weeks away.

The military was being rewarded with food and favor, prior to the beginning of Hitler's expected bold advancements beyond Austria, Poland and France, which had already been conquered by the Fuhrer's aggressions.

The invasion of England and possibly Russia appeared to be on Hitler's priority list.

Jews and Polish young women had been rounded up for sexual use by their special officers.

The program began in Berlin and had spread to outlying areas.

CHAPTER SIX

The local military on the campus had announced that female accompaniment would become available the following week.

Each officer would be assigned a woman for his pleasure, for three days, beginning on Friday.

Rules would be given prior to their arrival.

Hermann was enraged by the announcement. He could not envision such a forced episode involving a poor captured woman, without her personal consent.

He didn't know what to do about it. "I will contact my sister Ida," he told himself.

They would meet outside the hospital two hours later.

Ida had heard about this program in Berlin and never thought it would arrive at their location.

She also heard that the girls would be used and then killed when they became useless to the officers.

"We must do something", she told Hermann. "1 will consider helping you... but we must be very careful," she continued.

"Could you possibly hide the woman who might be assigned to me?" he returned.

"Yes, I will attempt to find a way to do it. I will contact you when I have found a way," she responded.

Hermann and Ida knew that huge penalties, or possibly death, could be awaiting them if they were caught in such an act. Yet, they had determination to do some personal good against this horrible national program which had been forced upon them.

Anna was guided towards room 212.

She arrived in her new prison uniform, without hair or cosmetics of any kind.

The thought of being raped by a Nazi officer turned her stomach. Yet, what could one do about it?

The girls had been told about not cooperating with the assigned officer. Punishment would not be lightly enforced.

She knew that she must cooperate or face terrible penalty, maybe even losing her life.

The door opened. There stood a six-foot young officer in military uniform.

He had a smile, and spoke with confidence, "I am Hermann, a medical officer and I have been told that you are Anna, yes?"

"Yes, I am Anna, just sixteen years-old from Belarus, Poland. I understand and speak German," she said.

She continued, "I have not had any sexual experiences, nor have I had any desire to participate in any until I meet someone who might love me, and I love him."

Hermann responded, "It is interesting that you should say that... because I feel the same way. Based on that information, I assure you that you are safe with me during these three days that you have been assigned here."

"Wow," she returned. "If you treat me that way, I will be forever grateful, at least."

He came back, "please sit down and tell me of your background and family."

Anna, in her amazement, sat down on the edge of his bed and began to tell of her family and what had happened to them.

She included her own personal background, growing up in Poland, and her plight to get where she had arrived.

Hermann listened closely as she recited her history and updated information.

He couldn't keep from noticing her confidence, command of the German language, and overall intelligence.

Matching all of this was her outward beauty – her protruding eyes, the shape of her nose and ears, and lovely parting lips. She was a perfect example of youth and loveliness.

He was, in a way, mesmerized by her presentation.

Soon, it would be his turn to tell of his background.

CHAPTER SEVEN

She listened intensely to his background, his personal dislike of the Fuhrer's actions, and about his forced induction into the German military.

He spoke of his family's outrage with the taking of Jews from the community.

Being just twenty-three years old, he told of his alliance with his sister Ida and how they were determined to find a way to help targeted individuals, like Anna, that could become torched or eliminated by the German military.

"Surprised, my sister Ida and I thought that you would most likely be a Jew. But even though you are Christian, our longing to help you has not changed.

Our family is Lutheran, as you might expect. We believe in all religions and their rights to worship the way they desire.

Ida and I have already begun planning to attempt to save you.

The actual plans will develop soon, and we will discuss them with you in time".

Anna now realized, more than ever, how lucky she was at this point. "Could this really be true, or am I dreaming?" she thought.

Meanwhile, Hermann couldn't take his eyes off her.

He began to blush at the serious attention that he was bestowing on this young beauty.

Hermann had never focused on a female, except his sister and mother. "What could be happening?" he thought.

It became obvious that this girl had become desirable. Yet, he had made a promise to treat her safely and he was truly a man of his word.

Anna was also beginning to fall for Hermann. His presentation and softness brought her to thinking in that direction.

There was a knock on the door.

It was lunch and the young soldier who delivered it had a wonderful smile on his face.

The lunch consisted of beef patties, a small potato, a pickle, a cup of soup, and a small piece of cake.

They sat across from each other on the bed and consumed the luncheon.

Anna noted that this was among the best daytime lunch plates she had received in a long time.

Soon after the meal, they returned to sharing their stories with one another.

It continued until darkness, when both began showing their fatigue.

Hermann announced that he was about to wash and go to bed. He then offered to wait until she might consider doing the same.

Anna walked to the bathroom area and slowly began to wash.

When both had completed the preparation, they were ready for bed.

"I promised you protection from sexual advancement and I will keep that promise," he stated.

"You have already gone beyond expectations and promise," Anna responded.

The large bed received their bodies and sleep quickly overtook them.

It was evident that the excitement of the day stayed with them during this first night's sleep together.

Breakfast and dinner from the night before were waiting at their door. It had been delivered last evening and this morning's breakfast was still warm.

Last night's evening meal consisted of a large roast chicken, slices of sweet potato and beans. A cookie was included on a separate plate.

CHAPTER EIGHT

W hen they awoke in the morning, they were wrapped around each other.

Anna couldn't believe that she had ended up in his arms. Hermann felt the same.

"I promised and did not touch you. It was nice, however, to begin the morning in each other's arms," he exclaimed.

"This was the best sleep I've had since being dragged from home, long ago," she returned.

She continued, "You are a gentleman and I am overwhelmed by the politeness and gentleness that you have exhibited to me. My mother instilled in me to someday find a man possessing your characteristics. She also warned me that such a man would be very hard to find in the world that I have been put into".

Hermann responded, "Thank you for your encouragement and honesty. I continue to be impressed by you, in so many ways. Let's wash and dress, breakfast will surely be knocking, or it may already be left outside our door," he finished.

The Nazis had stripped Anna of her usual clothes and she was forced to wear her prisoner uniform. There was no underwear or supports issued, just a working uniform with one pair of pants.

Even though she had been given a fresh uniform back at the sorority house, it was still just pants and a shirt.

The previous night, after washing, she had taken off the shirt and pants and came to bed in the nude. Hermann had just underwear on when entering the bed on his side.

In the darkness Herman couldn't see the nude body of Anna. But, when she arose from the bed in the morning, her youthful figure was immediately put before him.

"My God, you are even more beautiful in the flesh than I could have imagined. I can see why boys and men would want to engage you. But your head and brains are more important than one's body. Please get washed and dressed. I look forward to continuing our discussions," he responded.

They washed and dressed and found their breakfast outside the door.

CHAPTER
NINE

Pebbles bounced off the rear window of the apartment.

"It is my sister Ida. She wants me to come down the back staircase and meet her outside. She cannot enter this building, and if she did, both of us would be in big trouble. I must go and meet with her now. Please just relax. I will return in a few minutes."

His sister Ida had a plan.

It was already the second day. She wanted to institute the plan that night or chance the third evening.

Hermann stated immediately, "I cannot execute the plan tonight. Tomorrow night will have to do. I need more time with Anna, the girl. She will explain to you why we need that extra time."

Ida began to detail her plan.

"Your woman is to sneak down the back steps at midnight, not sooner. She is to go behind the bushes and shrubs encompassing the trash receptacles. There, she will find my bicycle, which l am leaving right now. Wrapped around the frame structure is a borrowed dress and scarf for her to change into. She should put her prison uniform in a trash barrel there, burying it deep into the barrel. With this dress and scarf around her head, she is to bike to the outer gate of the campus. You must give her confidence on the route.

Every evening at midnight the guards exchange places. Also, workers in the kitchen and maids go home at that time, as well. Several will be departing and arriving by bike for her to mix with. Just outside the campus entering gate is a small park, across the street. There, she is to ditch the bike and meet up with me. The two of us will then walk back to the hospital and into my room.

My hospital is located about three miles away from this fraternity house, but only about one and a half miles from the entrance gate. If everything goes right, this plan should take about 40 minutes to complete. I will take her from this point on. You must feign ignorance about her missing. They will investigate and find very little. No one could involve you... or me. From this point on we cannot communicate until several weeks have gone by. We must break up this meeting now to avoid suspicion."

He immediately kissed Ida and went back up the stairs to room 212.

When Hermann reentered the room, Anna was lying back on the bed.

"Is everything alright?" she blurted.

"Yes, my sister has planned your escape. I will tell you all the details later," he returned.

They finished the barely warm breakfast. Hermann continued showing his affection toward Anna.

"If only this war would end. I could picture your hair returning to your scalp. It would be radiant and well coifed to complement your overall loveliness. I wish that I could take you to Berlin, Paris, London, and Rome to buy you dresses and accessories to make you a spectacular model. I am dreaming of such pleasure. Is it obvious that I am falling for you, and I don't know how to handle it."

Anna responded, "With what I have been through it is difficult for me to face your wonderful handling of my situation. I still have insecurities about my future and history of the loss of my family. But you have made me begin to come out of this shell and have caused me to appreciate humans once again. I do have great affection for you, and I think that I may be in love with you. My body clings to the warmth of your body from last night. I think I'm beginning to get a woman's urge to reach out to you. Please continue to go easy with me," she completed.

With that they returned to the side of the bed where they had been talking for almost a full day.

"Maybe I should request a kiss from you, if you are interested," she continued.

Hermann wasted no time, pushed forward, and placed a meaningful kiss upon her naked lips. She wouldn't let go.

Anna whispered, "Thank you" in his ear and returned to her lips for more.

They kissed and kissed and fell back on the bed.

Though they were dressed, their bodies came together.

"Please, wait until tonight," she pleaded.

"Of course," he replied.

The afternoon continued with information, holding hands and an occasional kiss.

They had clearly reached an important step in their relationship. Their excitement became obvious.

The night couldn't come fast enough.

CHAPTER TEN

They had put aside their evening meal.

Instead, they romantically began to undress each other.

Both in the nude, they pounced upon the bed, wrapping arms, once again, around each other.

Smothered by kisses, their emotions overtook their meeting.

Anna waited with anticipation, to follow his lead to sexual intercourse. She had thought that she was ready.

Without experience Hermann's body began to expand with excitement. He now knew that she was waiting, and he slowly brought his mouth to her skin, exploring his young woman's neck, breasts and womanly areas.

It was a thrill he had never thought of experiencing.

Anna too had kissed his neck and chest, arms, and further. They had reached the peak of sexual readiness.

He mounted her and carefully worked his manhood into her warm and moist opening.

They both let out cries.

Anna, though hurting from the invasion, knew that she had reached the emotional height of this man's affection... and it was somehow wonderful.

Hermann, who without proper teaching, realized that he had completed his capture of this wonderful woman, of whom he was in love with. It was this wonderful satisfaction that he had never attained before in his young life.

Although still in some sort of pain, she didn't want him to come out of her.

They tossed and turned, without breaking their ties, kissing and tonguing as their bodies moved.

Throughout the night they continued their emotional releases like most couples never get to do.

It was true love, at its finest.

Unfortunately, the sun rose, and morning was upon them.

Hermann told her of the plan.

They now realized that this could be their last day together -- their last day ever.

Tonight, they were to attempt the escape plan that his sister Ida had formulated.

CHAPTER
ELEVEN

Anna was now in tears.

She had suddenly realized that her new lover may not survive the war and she, herself, might not make it through either.

"Will we ever be together again?" she asked him

Hermann returned, "It will be in God's hands. We must not give up trying to survive and to find each other."

He continued, "My sister Ida has confidence in her plan, and we must attempt it. We have no other alternatives.

If we don't try, you will be taken away and eventually eliminated, as we are told. I cannot let that happen.

This is my only chance to save you. We must take it... tonight."

He paused and continued, "My sister Ida is wonderful. You will immediately love her, as I do. She is intelligent and creative and will surely protect you with her own life, if need be.

She does not know of our love for each other. However, she is curious and suspects something, particularly since I demanded we needed the extra day together.

I am sure that she will get to love you, like I have, quite quickly. You two will make great friends, as family.

Please God, I am hopeful that Ida will find the way to save you for me.

As for myself, I too am in God's hands, for I do not know where or when I will be expected to play doctor. But I have no choice.

I promise you that I will do anything possible to survive, for you and for a future with you... for eternity. I love you so much."

He immediately embraced her, clearing away her tears.

Anna contributed, "Let's enjoy the remaining hours of this important day together," and she wrapped her arms around him tightly.

CHAPTER TWELVE

Anna chose to trace his face with her hands, examining his special features and she put her hands through his thick, brown, wavy hair.

She wanted to forever remember his eyes, nose and ears. His mouth she would never need to think about, as it would remain with her, always.

Hermann couldn't get enough of her passion, beauty, and intelligence.

He promised to always remember her face and her envisioned hair having returned to her bare scalp. "You will be in my dreams forever," he blurted.

In between these long and important examinations of each other, they once again met in sexual intercourse.

Their climatic releases were followed by continual emotions of love for each other. They repeated their feelings for the remaining hours of the day.

Eventually, darkness fell upon them.

They were to eat one final meal together.

Beside the outer door was a platter of fowl (turkey or chicken) with gravy and carrots on a second dish. Two apples were included for dessert. A vial of tea leaned next to the plate.

Hermann made a toast to his love, "I pray for your successful escape from here to the arms of my sister Ida. May God guide you safely."

Anna returned, "I too pray, not only for my own survival, but for the love of my young life, who has given me reason to survive, to again meet up with me... so we may live our remaining years together in peace."

After finishing dinner, they fell asleep in each other's arms.

Hermann knew he must awake before midnight in time to give his final goodbye to Anna as she left his room, in the first step of the plan.

CHAPTER THIRTEEN

Hermann had risen from his sleep and finally had to shake Anna awake to prepare for the escape.

It was eleven-forty-five, and in fifteen minutes or less she was to begin the plan.

He hugged her during her rise to her feet, and he bent for his final kiss.

She squeezed him with all her might. Then, she looked into his eyes to say her final goodbye.

"I have trust and faith in you and your sister, and I will give the escape my very best effort. I will never forget our time together. It has been the most important happening in my young life. I thank God that I have found my man. Please, be safe and return to me. I will be waiting."

Anna straitened her shirt and pants and walked slowly to the door.

She walked through the door and fought the urge to turn around and see him one last time.

The sounds of her steps down the stairs were barely audible. She entered the outside quietly.

Hermann was a mess. He didn't know what to do.

His love had left on a dangerous attempt of escape, and he would probably not discover whether she was successful or not for several weeks, if at all.

He didn't even know whether he would be around to ever find out the truth.

"I must find a way to divert my concerns and to get back to sleep," he told himself.

"We were not allowed a radio and so I will read an old Berlin newspaper that was in this room when I arrived. I hope to distract my mind enough so sleep may come."

He did eventually fall asleep and the dawn of the morning arrived quickly.

Having completed the third evening of the program, German officers would be expecting the return of the young girls to the awaiting truck.

CHAPTER
FOURTEEN

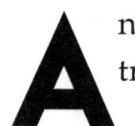nna found the trash can, the bushes, and trees.

Around the back of the trash, protected by overgrown bushes, was the used bicycle.

As promised, attached to the bars, were a folded simple maiden's dress and a black scarf, hanging from the lower part of the dress.

Anna quickly disrobed and changed into the necessary clothes.

The dress was several sizes too big and the scarf smelled of a toiletry that was not very pleasant. But it would have to do.

She had not ridden a bike for several years, but the pedals and seat seemed adequate.

There being no advanced gears, its movement appeared simple and reliable for her.

Biking along the back of the fraternity house to the street was easy.

She turned and continued her ride toward the campus gates.

Within minutes she spotted individuals walking in the same direction.

Two vehicles came along the same road, also heading toward the campus entrances. Finally, another bike appeared just ahead.

She thought that the gates were just a few blocks more.

Suddenly, just ahead of her, a Nazi soldier came out from the right and entered the street before her.

"Achtung!" he shouted, and he motioned for her to stop just front of him.

"Haben se eine cigarette, Frauline?" he inquired.

"Nicht," Anna returned, in perfect German.

"Danke." he replied. "Ar vedasame."

Anna continued biking toward the gates.

She crossed under the arch and through the gates with a vehicle and several walkers around her.

The timing appeared to be excellent. She success-fully exited the military campus as planned.

Across from the gated area was indeed a small park with thick large trees. She made her way into the park.

Waiting at the far end of the small park was a fig-ure of a woman, who just might be Ida.

Anna brought her bike to the other end of the park to dispose of it behind a series of large oak trees.

She leaned the bike against the back of the thickest tree and proceeded to walk around the group of trees.

Waiting for her was Hermann's sister Ida.

"Please don't talk, just follow me. Hold my hand." Ida requested.

They walked the extra one and a half miles to the hospital complex.

As they mounted the rear housing area together, it appeared that the initial escape plan had been successful.

CHAPTER FIFTEEN

Back at the fraternity house, an officer called the names of the returning women of the weekend program off a clipboard.

He called three times the name, "Anna Kanopsky."

The officer blew his whistle and asked if anyone knew of her whereabouts.

With no response, he closed the truck door and locked it.

Immediately he spoke into his handy microphone that was given to him for such emergencies.

Within minutes more Nazi guards arrived at the vehicle.

The truck officer gave information about the missing woman to the leader of the guards.

Two military trucks followed, loaded with trained soldiers to begin the search for the missing woman.

For the rest of that Monday, the campus was searched from building to building and street to street.

Three Nazis visited Room 212 and spoke to Hermann Berger, as expected.

They appeared convinced that Hermann had nothing to do with Anna's escape.

He told of his wonderful weekend with her and that she had left early Monday morning, as they had been instructed.

Without hesitation, he mentioned that she had thanked him for everything, and he was of the belief that she was headed to the awaiting truck.

They soon left the building. Hermann was relieved. His focus returned to Anna and Ida. Had they made it?

Two days later, Hermann was given his expected formal orders.

It stated that he was to be ready to leave the college campus at noon the day after tomorrow.

They were to send a vehicle to pick him up, and he would be transported by train to Bremen, Germany for work in a newly established battlefield hospital.

There he was to work under the Command of Marshal Doctor Lars Von See. Personal items would not be allowed.

Hermann immediately went down the hall to the first room and knocked on the door.

Dr. Elgrid Hacker had been assigned to that room. Hermann had met him in the training program just a week before.

On the door was a note intended for someone else. It indicated that he was being penalized for having mistreated his weekend woman, and that his whereabouts would not be made known for several weeks or longer.

Hermann had hoped that he might be available to take a note to the Dortmund Hospital for him as a parting favor.

Now, Hermann would have to find another person who could help deliver a note to Ida. It was to be the young soldier that delivered food each day to his building.

The soldier gladly accepted his note, understanding that Hermann had received his orders and was leaving the day after next.

Hermann offered him a financial gift, but the young man refused saying, "I am not
allowed to accept anything on my job. I would be held responsible if caught by my superiors. These are strict orders and I must follow them."

And so, Hermann was to leave for duty on Wednesday with the hope that Ida and Anna would receive his message.

He was now prepared to go to work for his country.

CHAPTER SIXTEEN

Ida had taken Anna to her room situated on the second floor of the worker's quarters attached to the Dortmund Hospital.

Her room consisted of a large bed, a used wooden dresser with a mirror, a chair, and a small closet. There was a rather large window next to the dresser and a used rug covered most of the floor in the room.

Two doors down the hall was a washroom with two sinks and a toilet. It was one of four washrooms in the wooden building. Ida had regarded it as "adequate."

Her complete setup appeared rather clean, safe, and warm.

The other girls in the building were mostly nurses and volunteers like Ida.

There was no indication of military or government influence within her group. She felt protected… so far.

Ida assured Anna that she should be quite safe within the room and could probably fit herself into the hospital program at some point.

"I will share my bed and everything with you without a problem. You will have to stay here for a while and then slowly work your way into our existing program. I will teach you the work slowly and carefully. Don't you worry," Ida explained to Anna.

The two women conversed in German, learning much about each other in a short time.

By the second morning, they had become trusted friends.

Anna began telling Ida of her affair with brother Hermann that had taken place in his room.

"We are both deeply in love. I have never met a man like him. He is the most generous, considerate, smart, and lovable male that I have known. I find him handsome, soft and irresistible. He has let himself become romantic and is full of wonderful emotions. His outward desire to save me was unexpected. I thought he was fooling. He brought me back to human acceptance, which I had lost back in Poland.

"We were attracted to each other instantly and fell in love and we want to spend the rest of our lives together. Please God, save us from this terrible war... and allow us to come together once again.

"Hermann promised that you and I would become family. He knew his orders would bring him close to battle and to danger. It is doubtful that he would hear your plan had worked and that I am safe, with you, for now. We must both pray for his safety and return home, for all our sakes."

Ida replied, "I am thrilled for Hermann that he has found his love. I can honestly see why he has picked you. And, as he had predicted, you and I are hereby "family." You have already made me happy! Hopefully, we can stay together throughout this war and be here waiting for Hermann's return."

CHAPTER SEVENTEEN

Dr. Von-See ordered Hermann to wrap the broken arm.

The patient was a field officer who had been injured during a tailgate drop in the rear of a supply vehicle.

Dr. Von-See set the arm in place and built a makeshift cast around the area. The cast needed to be wrapped with medical tape so that the broken pieces could, hopefully, bond.

Hermann proceeded to do the job.

Ships were arriving daily from war zones throughout Europe.

Each group brought different medical requirements.

Shrapnel from the enemy's return fire penetrated various parts of the soldier's bodies.

Individuals arriving required quick and professional addressing of their needs.

Dr. Von-See had been an optometrist in Colon when he was drafted into the Wehrmacht. He too did not have the medical training required of a proper doctor.

Two other doctors were attached to this medical location, one being a dentist and another an animal doctor, in training only, without credentials.

One female nurse was assigned to the group for help.

The activities of this group were to be "experimental" at best.

The latest arrival contained three soldiers, with blood either flowing or stained on their uniforms.

Dr. Von-See, who was in charge, selected both Hermann and the dentist, Dr. Kluge, to "do what you can" for the three soldiers.

Nurse Brendel was summoned to clean up their wounds. She dropped the hand-cleaning of medical tools into the basin from which she had been working.

She was a veteran nurse who had decent training in operations and possessed a sundry of medical skills, and she was a welcome addition to the group.

"It will only take a minute or two to clean them to some order," she responded. She began working on the soldier closest to her.

He screamed in pain as she wiped the blood from his fresh wound.

Hermann moved forward to examine the actual wound. "It is a crease to the shoulder. He will survive to see action once again," Hermann observed. "I will attempt to take out the bullet."

He reached for a pair of plyers to do the work.

"The culprit has come out. You will be well, quite soon," Hermann said to his patient.

The second soldier was unconscious. Blood had flowed all around him. He appeared to have been shot in the neck.

They lifted his body and discovered he was already dead. He had apparently perished during transit to the hospital.

The third man had blood pouring from his face.

The nurse began cleaning the blood from his face and realized that he too was dead.

Another stretcher had a soldier crying softly. His leg was dangling abnormally on his right side.

"Can we save his leg?" inquired Hermann.

"I have never stitched a severed leg like that, have you?" returned Dr. Von-See.

"Well, I will try to accomplish it today," Hermann committed. "Nurse, please prepare the patient for surgery."

And so, as an apprentice to the nurse's recommendations, Hermann performed his first operational endeavor.

Although the work was far from professional, he succeeded in saving the soldier's leg.

That patient was then transferred to a hospital in the interior of the German countryside.

Hermann and the others continued to struggle with the incoming casualties of war for nearly three years.

In August of 1944, they were bombed by Allied forces from the continual raids in the area.

One such raid hit the medical area injuring most of the individuals inside.

Dr. Hermann Berger lost his right arm in the explosion.

Despite the life-altering injury, he continued working to the best of his ability until the war finally came to a close.

His Germany had lost the war, and most of the country had been devastated by the Allies in retaliation.

Dr. Berger was, at last, finished with his work for Hitler in Bremen and began working his way home to Dortmund.

CHAPTER EIGHTEEN

Nazi soldiers back at the fraternity house continued searching for Anna Kanopsky.

They had no leads and so they began by reexamining any connections she made while there.

Although Dr. Hermann Berger was interrogated the day after Anna went missing, they wanted to double-check his story.

Two specialists departed toward Bremen by train.

A British fighter plane spotted the moving train and destroyed it.

Both specialists were killed in the incident.

Hermann was never interrogated a second time.

Anna's description, however, was posted in several locations within the general area. The officers hoped to find a lead with which to continue their search for the missing woman.

Ida spotted one of the post papers pinned to the college entrance advertisement board and became horrified. The thought of being discovered immediately penetrated her mind.

"I must change her appearance or move her to another location," she told herself. "I should probably do both."

During her time in Dortmund Hospital, Anna's appearance had already changed quite a bit. Her dirty blonde hair had begun to grow back from her scalp and only increased her beauty.

"Before long she will be able to pass as a German youth, but for now I must keep her under lock and key," Ida pondered. "I will continue bringing her food and looking after her closely."

Anna kept herself on the second floor mostly in Ida's room. Her visits to the washroom had to be well planned as she had to keep away from others who might be using the shared facilities.

It seemed to be working well.

By this time in the war, German authorities were intercepting all mail and correspondence.

Any correspondence to the hospital had to be inspected as well.

The note from Dr. Hermann Berger to his sister Ida was lying within a pile on the front entrance desk.

As promised, the young food delivery soldier had delivered the personal note addressed to Ida.

It had been inspected several days before.

The family name, Berger, caught the inspector's eyes.

He immediately reported it to Gestapo Headquarters.

It opened the girl's disappearance case once again.

The note read:

Dearest Sister Ida,

I have received my orders, which will take me far-away. My country needs my skills and I must go at once to help win our war.

Thank you for taking care of my personal things until I return home.

Please give my love to our friends and relatives that you may encounter while I am away.

I certainly hope and pray that I will be able to return home to once again be with you and our important family.

Auf Wiedersehen, Hermann

After reading the letter, the authorities decided to speak with Ida Berger. They wanted to know who their friends and important family members may be, as well as the nature of personal things she was supposed to be taking care of in her brother's absence.

A letter was given to the front desk requiring Ida to meet with the authorities next week at Gestapo headquarters.

When this letter was hand delivered to her, included was Hermann's note.

She began fearing the worst. "Why do they want me? Have they suspected a connection to Anna? I hope not," she told herself.

Upon hearing of Ida's future investigation, Anna began to cry.

"I can't have you facing any danger because of me. There must be another way out of this. Please, consider other options," Anna blurted.

CHAPTER NINETEEN

The Gestapo agent Claus Smidt who had been assigned to the Anna Kanopsky case, had just received a hand delivered letter from Berlin.

The letter requested his transfer to a border location within Holland. His expertise appeared to be needed in the deportation of Jews from the Netherlands.

The orders demanded his arrival within twenty-four hours.

Agent Smidt appointed Agent Wilma Strauss to take over the Anna Kanopsky case.

When Ida arrived for interrogation, she was sent to the third floor of Gestapo headquarters.

Agent Wilma Strauss was waiting and immediately began questioning her.

"In the note from Heir Dr. Berger, your brother, he mentions your friends. Who was he referring to?" she requested.

"Here in Dortmund we have had many friends over the years most of whom are now serving the Fuhrer." Ida responded.

"Well then, who are your important family members?" the agent continued relentlessly.

"They are my parents. Both are working in the airplane factory in North Dortmund," Ida returned.

"Then, he mentions that you had taken care of his personal things, yes? What are those personal things?"

"I had closed out his personal bank account of 14 marks and returned two books to the library for him. One was *Mein Kampf,*" she offered and prayed the agent wouldn't be able to call her bluff.

"Well, that is very good. You may go. We are sorry to have bothered you, but we are still searching for the missing Polish woman, and of course we will continue to do so." The agent finished.

Ida left Gestapo headquarters relieved, to say the least.

When she opened the door to her room Anna ran into her arms.

"They accepted my answers and immediately released me. I think we are safe, for now," Ida blurted.

"Thank God. I was worried that you would not return! Thank God, once again," Anna cried.

Ida and Anna slept well that evening.

The next day seemed bright and cheerful. They had managed to avoid an obstacle that had been placed before them without warning.

The war's ending was getting closer each day. Yet, the German public was told that they were winning the war, despite the daily Allied bombing raids that had begun to destroy all their country.

CHAPTER TWENTY

Germany had been systematically destroyed

They had now received a token of the retaliation that they rightfully deserved.

Key cities had been wiped out and most factories blown up.

Communications were major targets and had been eliminated.

Airfields were among the first to be demolished.

All military locations were precision bombed.

The remnants of war were everywhere and affected everyone – native, ally, or enemy.

Those who were fortunate enough to have survived arose, some from beneath the rubble, and some from the acute destruction that stretched in all directions.

The streets were cluttered with debris, broken vehicles, armaments, and most horrifyingly, dead bodies.

There was no chance of assembling order on the horizon.

It was obvious the war was over, and Germany had been utterly defeated.

Movement would be slow with a hopeful new trust in government of the people.

Would forgiveness come to them? Would peace prevail?

Germany, as a country, must survive. The conquering Allies must see to it.

Several world leaders met in Malta to approve the apparent moves that would be necessary to re-build Germany, the rest of destroyed Europe, and surrounding territories.

They decided that thousands of prisoners of war must be allowed to return to their homes. (Unfortunately, not all of them were released.)

Dr. Hermann Berger, who had served the Third Reich, the best he knew how, had lost his right arm in the conflicts.

He left Bremen in a small military Volkswagen with his friend, Litvick, who did the driving.

Litvick was from Colon. He was a cook who had received burns on most of his body in the same explosion that maimed Hermann.

After the explosion, he was unable to wear clothing, for the most part, and even today, he was dressed in just priority pants and hat for identification purposes.

He could still drive, and the vehicle had been located close by and was in pretty decent shape to the pair's pleasant surprise. The fuel, however, was more difficult to obtain.

As a youngster, Litvick had worked at a petrol station and learned how to siphon gasoline from junk trucks.

Sure enough, just a block away was a destroyed German tank. With a small piece of hose and a sundry bottle, Litvick was able to transfer the vital fuel from the tank into their waiting vehicle.

It got the military Volkswagen's engine perking.

Hermann and Litvick were to travel through military barriers at every juncture where identification was needed.

The barrier soldiers were mostly British and American.

Food was scarcely available during the long trip, and Hermann and Litvick were very hungry.

Along a road heading south was a farm that had been taken over by the Nazis. It now had a sign in German that read, "Essen Now."

Fresh cooked cow meat was cut, and along with brown bread enabled a sandwich to be made quite quickly. Local wine complimented the collation.

Between them they were able to leave a handful of German coins in exchange for their meal, out of the generosity of their hearts.

That food would have to sustain them until they made it home.

They had a long way yet to get to Dortmund, and then further on to Colon for Litvick.

CHAPTER
TWENTY-ONE

The military Volkswagen was signaled to stop.

A group of Allied soldiers approached the vehicle.

They requested identification and asked the gentlemen to step out of the German military vehicle.

Two British soldiers dropped to the ground around it, looking underneath. Another U.S.

Army soldier looked under the seats and examined the interior.

A Russian soldier spoke fluent German and told Hermann and Litvick that a German vehicle rigged with explosives had crashed into a Russian truck killing nine men.

The soldiers had been ordered to check vehicles at any nearby barriers and intersections from that point on.

"You are clean and can proceed, carefully," the Russian soldier informed them.

Hermann and Litvick jumped back into the vehicle and sped away in a different direction.

Just ahead was a Russian flag, half bent, barely hanging above a smashed tank.

Litvick stopped and retrieved the colorful flag. He believed that it would make a fine addition to any collectible remnants of the war.

He had told Hermann that the Volkswagen would hopefully become his.

The vehicle needed three new tires, a new wind-shield – the present one being cracked – the torn seats needed repair, one head light was missing, and the wiper blades needed to be replaced.

The body, though, seemed to be in rather good shape, with only minor scratches and paint stripped in several places. The engine and trans-mission appeared to barely used.

Litvick viewed the vehicle as an asset, possibly his only asset, at the time. "Maybe this vehicle is my stroke of new luck," he rejoiced.

Hermann smiled during the summation. They were finally nearing Dortmund.

Although the buildings and surroundings had been mostly leveled, it reminded Hermann of old territory before the war began. He grew increas-ingly excited with each passing mile.

What would he find in his hometown? Had his mother and father survived? What about Ida and of course, his dear Anna?

Had his homestead made it through the war?

What will come of them all?

Yes, they were a defeated country at the mercy of the victors.

The answers to most of his questions laid just ahead.

"Might God give us a second chance?" he asked Litvick.

The military Volkswagen sped on towards the entrance to what would be left of the city of Dortmund, Germany.

CHAPTER TWENTY-TWO

Anna was not feeling well. Ida didn't exactly know what to do.

She had received Nurse training for only a year at the hospital and thought she might try aspirin which was, miraculously, still available in the building.

Two aspirin did nothing to improve Anna's condition, however.

Ida asked several of her nurses, referring to a patient that she once had before coming to the hospital.

One nurse responded, "Could she be pregnant?"

Ida was taken aback by the remark.

Sure enough... Anna was indeed pregnant with her brother's child!

"Wow! I guess you did sleep with him, didn't you?" she shouted.

"Yes, and I won't ever regret it... and I will be thrilled to deliver his baby into our lives," she returned.

"This will create another problem for us here in this room. I will need to steal more food, for you and now for the baby... and then attempt to deliver the child here as well.

"Keeping the baby here will be, especially without drawing attention, will be critical to our safety!"

"But... I will do it, as we will love the baby together," Ida gave in. "I'm thrilled to think that I'll have a nephew or a niece. Will you come up with names?" she wondered.

"Yes, if it is a boy, I will name him Luz after my father. If it is a girl, I will name it after my mother, Beatrice with a middle name of Ida after you." Anna answered and smiled up at Ida.

Ida responded once again, "I am so happy for you, your baby, and for Hermann! May he return safely to enjoy his child with us."

Some eight months later, Ida helped Anna deliver a beautiful, healthy baby boy, Luz, named after Anna's father who has perished at the very beginnings of the war.

CHAPTER TWENTY-THREE

The entrance to Dortmund was not so pleasant.

Damaged equipment seemed to be everywhere. Tanks and mobile artillery were scattered in the streets.

Pieces of armament clogged the main thoroughfare into the city proper.

Many people could be observed walking through rubble, attempting to find the remnants of their former lives.

It was not a great welcoming for Hermann to his beloved hometown.

Most of the buildings in the center were down to mortar and ashes.

The City Hall, the armory, the lecture center, the market area, and the homes surrounding the outskirts of the city were all practically eliminated.

The main road to the college campus was blocked off. There were huge holes and equipment holding back movement down this once important route.

Hermann asked Litvick to return to the center and take another back route. He was hoping that the alternative road would be open enough to allow them to reach the campus.

The bodies of the poorly departed were seen at several intervals along the route.

Hermann could see there was much to be done in Dortmund; just to clean up the remnants of human losses would be a serious undertaking.

He was beginning to doubt the survival of any of his loved ones as he and Litvik carefully made their way toward his family home site.

The college campus had been leveled. Only the entrance gate remained in original condition. They drove on.

His family strassa had been destroyed. The house where the Berger's once lived was down to its foundation. Brick and wood from the house lay around in pieces.

His bicycle seat was spotted under a fallen tree at the corner of the lot. Ida's favorite stuffed tiger was ripped to pieces, abandoned among the debris.

Thankfully, there were no bodies here. "Maybe they were moved to a safe location?" Hermann asked aloud, trying to convince himself.

"I will check with the churches and survivors on the streets, and anywhere else there may be information about my family.

"Litvick, I cannot hold you here any longer. You must leave at once. I cannot thank you enough for taking me home. God speed, and good luck." He embraced his friend.

The military Volkswagen perked and then sped off into the dust heading for the big city of Colon further down the Rhein River.

Hermann, wearing his class-A German officer's uniform, and carrying a small case with his shaving gear, toothbrush and paste, brush and comb,

began walking toward the Dortmund
Hospital which had miraculously survived the Allied bombing.

Yes, the hospital smartly had an "H" painted on
the roof top hoping to survive the constant bombing.

CHAPTER TWENTY-FOUR

The Dortmund Hospital received word that the war had come to a close. They had dodged the bombing and survived without a scratch.

All personnel were given the day off except for volunteers – they were needed to keep the patients under control until the nurses and doctors returned.

Most of the personnel began searching for relatives and friends who may have survived the onslaught.

Ida was a volunteer. She had to work to keep everyone happy.

Her mother, Ima Berger, had run from her house to the hospital when the bombing started. She was lucky because their family house received massive damage shortly after she had fled.

The hospital accepted many fleeing individuals, several with children.

Along with Ida's mother Ima, many had to sleep on the floors.

Ida couldn't improve the situation. At least her mother was safe, though. She was thankful for that.

Her dad, Borden Berger, had been chosen right from the factory to go to Bremerhaven to help in the production of field mines.

The field mine factory had been selected by British bombers and took many a hit during the last week of the conflict.

Borden Berger injured his back and shoulders. Shrapnel and explosives had punished his body. A young man without medical training was doctoring the casualties that had previously taken explosions in several nearby buildings. Luckily, he was able to save Borden's life.

The Berger family had not heard from Borden in nearly a month and concern had risen to the point that her mother wanted to go immediately and search for him.

"Father and Hermann are smart enough to know that the hospital may have been saved. They would surely attempt to contact us... if possible. We must wait here for a good amount of time and see if anything arrives from them," Ida conveyed to her mother.

When the announcement that the war was over finally reached her, Ida opened her bedroom door and led Anna and son Luz out of their long captivity hideaway.

Anna and the baby, now nearly two years old, were playing on the floor in the adjacent room.

It was obvious that everyone in the facility no longer cared about those new faces who had been living in Ida's room.

Everyone was grappling with the loss of the war.

There was relief but no merriment among them.

Ida, her mother, Anna, and the baby knew they must wait to see if any others of their family had managed to survive.

CHAPTER TWENTY-FIVE

Hermann's face was filthy. He needed a shave badly.

His uniform was torn at the waist and worn at the collar. It had stains down the front areas and the pleats were gone from its pressing.

He had worn this uniform for several days straight and was in it when the first explosion came his way.

When his arm caught the enemy fire, followed by the gigantic explosion, he was bleeding next to the open bones.

Dr. Von-See immediately severed what was remaining of the hanging lines connecting his shoulder to the arm. He plugged up the stump with cotton and cloth to solidify the formed stump.

Hermann was given medicine to calm the pain and he drifted into sleep

Several others in the medical tent were hurt as well.

The tent itself was blown to bits and the limited medical area was left open to the enemy.

Most of the tent individuals began scattering in several directions.

Two hours later, they were informed that the war had been lost, and that Germany had surrendered.

Litvick told Hermann he was going to attempt to go home. "Want to come home with me?" he shouted.

Hermann returned quickly, "Find a way and I'm with you! I live in Dortmund. I know you live in Colon. You could drop me off along the way, somehow."

And so, here he is approaching the Dortmund Hospital after walking about three miles from the demolished site of his family home.

Adding to his awful looks were dust and debris from the ride in Litvick's open military Volkswagen.

He climbed the two front steps to the entrance of the hospital.

There in front of him, just ten feet away, sat his sister Ida.

She looked up from her desk to see this disheveled military creature. It took her a few moments to realize it was her beloved brother.

"Is it really you, Hermann? It must be!" she shouted.

Then she screamed at the top of her lungs.

Two other volunteers reacted to the scream and ran to her side.

"This is my brother, Hermann. He is the most important man in my life."

She ran to him and they embraced like never before.

"My God, you have been injured! What has happened?" she asked.

Hermann answered, "I lost my arm in an explosion, but I am otherwise alright. Were you able to save my Anna?" he demanded.

"Yes, and she is in the next room, to the left of the stairs. Be prepared for a surprise." Ida smiled at him.

Hermann straightened up his battered tie and walked immediately to the room.

There, on the floor was Anna, playing with a young boy.

"I have somehow survived. And I am here to claim the love of my dreams." he blurted.

Anna dropped the toy soldier in her hand and rushed to him in excitement.

They melted together like the two lost souls that they had been, with tears running down their cheeks.

"God has saved both of us. We can never repay Him. I prayed and prayed that somehow we both would survive this terrible war... and we have," Anna sobbed into Hermann's shoulder.

"I love you. I never lost faith in God that we would once again return to each other," he whispered to her.

"What has happened to your arm?" she exclaimed.

"An explosion blew it from my shoulder. I have a stump, but I am otherwise medically fine. Please don't let my loss ruin our reunion. Remember, I love you and I won't let this loss stand in the way of our life together," he ended.

Anna broke away from his arms, "And this is our son." Anna gestured to the small boy still playing on the floor. "Yes, our son, Luz, named after my father. He has your sister's nose, and your eyes and spark. When you get a chance to clean up, he would love to meet his father. Please go up the stairs to the second floor. You'll find the washroom stocked with plenty of soap and maybe even a razor. In the meantime, I will ask the volunteer nurses if any clothes have been left in the doctors' offices. If there are, hopefully, they will fit you well enough."

With that recommendation, he grabbed her once again and they embraced for a second time.

He then turned and immediately went to the stairs and began to climb to the second floor.

God's favor for this reunion will never be forgotten. Only God could have made this possible, Hermann thought. Other survivors will not fare as well.

CHAPTER TWENTY-SIX

Ida, her brother, and her mother were all together once again.

But what about the family patriarch?

Borden Berger left Bremerhaven where he had been badly injured.

He had jumped upon a military truck that had survived the war, along with ten others trying to make their way toward home or elsewhere.

A short distance into the journey, they were stopped by a group of armed Russian soldiers at an intersection that had been blocked off due to road conditions.

In the Russian language, an officer demanded that two of the passengers from the truck remain at the intersection with them.

They picked two passengers, one of them being Borden Berger. The truck driver was motioned to continue.

Borden had no choice but to remain with the Russian soldiers.

Borden and the other German passenger were quickly put into a Russian military vehicle and driven off in another direction.

Two years were to pass before he was finally released by the Russians.

Borden Berger was treated quite well because, as the Russians soon found out, he was very intelligent. Both men, however, were captives of the Russian government during their stay.

They were not allowed to write or communicate with friends or family during their captivity.

When finally released, transportation had become available, and the two boarded a train headed for Paris, France.

There, they found another train to Colon, Germany.

While in Paris they were able to send communications to Germany.

The Berger family was thrilled to hear that Borden had somehow survived. They had given up waiting for word, either from him or about him.

It was now 1947 and most of the roads had been cleared. Sections of cities destructed during the war had begun to open up once again.

Construction was everywhere. Survivors were working in the reconstruction, and new life was beginning to show itself throughout Germany.

Ida and her mother departed Dortmund by train to hopefully meet up with her father.

They had received a message that he would be arriving in Colon within the next two days. Ima wanted desperately to be there for his arrival.

Hermann, Anna, and Luz would be anxiously waiting back in Dortmund.

It appeared that, finally, the whole Berger family would be reunited.

CHAPTER
TWENTY-SEVEN

Back at the Dortmund Hospital, Dr. Hermann Berger, his lover Anna, and their two-year-old son Luz had been using their time to get reacquainted with one another.

Hermann and Anna once again recaptured the love which began blooming at the beginning of the war. They renewed all the commitments they made to each other when they first became lovers.

Anna wanted to formally marry Hermann and they decided to do it as soon as possible. "When your father returns, we shall be ready to finalize the plans," Anna announced.

"Yes, my parents and sister will be delighted!" Hermann returned.

Meanwhile, Hermann and Luz had become great play pals, and the love between father and son was evident.

Hermann, because of his handicap, could not officially work. He had registered for a military disabled stipend and had already received several of its monthly payments.

Thankfully, these funds were enough to support the whole family as other income was very limited during these early post-war times.

The hospital offered Dr. Hermann a temporary job of examining the continuing line of injured people from the area who were connected to the war and needed physical and mental help.

The actual work was completed by other doctors and nurses on the hospital staff.

For his effort, he and his family were given most of the second floor of the rear building that housed the nurses and volunteers.

The second day had come and gone without word from his mother or sister. Did they get to Colon? Had his father arrived? Were they on their way back to Dortmund?

Finally, on day three, the front door to the hospital swung open and in walked his mother and father with his sister Ida.

Father was a mess. He had lost most of his hair and aged quite a bit. His face needed a shave. The rest of his body required a good bath and clean clothes.

Hermann immediately embraced his father, both with tears in their eyes. His mother began crying, also.

Ida enjoyed watching them reunite, smiling.

The Russians had not bothered with his looks.

Soon they all settled down to hear father's story of what happened to him during the last two years.

He spoke clearly of the work he had done for the war, in the factory, under the close supervision of the Gestapo agents.

When he was picked to go to Bremerhaven, he was warned about his behavior at the new job.

Two men who had held the same position had been dismissed and punished.

One was hung outside on a lamppost. The other was shot outside against a wall, next to the building.

He was to build field mines which were to be used to kill the enemies.

After hearing the end use of the product he was manufacturing, he quickly realized why the previous two workers did not cooperate.

Borden made the difficult choice of complying with the Gestapo agents and was obedient in making the field mines. He would do anything possible to get back to his family.

When Allied bombers started bombing the area, the factory was evacuated. But when the kitchen staff refused to leave their work, they were shot while in the kitchen and anyone who did not die was left to endure the bombing.

The Gestapo agents started firing at the rest of the workers.

Borden caught shrapnel in his back and shoulders.

Thankfully, the British air attack continued toward the factory and the Gestapo agents were forced to flee for their own lives.

Soon after it was announced that the war was over.

He and his co-workers began to leave the area, some on foot, others by bike or by military vehicles that had somehow survived the war.

Borden and two of his friends jumped onto the back of a truck heading towards Colon.

When he was picked by the Russian soldiers, he was taken to an encampment which he believed was outside of Moscow. He was held there for nearly two years after the end of the war.

The Russians took reasonable care of him, though, because he became of great use to them.

They regularly talked to him, seeking information on field mines and his knowledge of the factory work that he had completed. He was even able to help with some emergency medical situations that presented themselves at the encampment, which impressed the Russians.

When they finally released him, Russia and the surrounding countries had already begun rebuilding.

Fortunately, some transportation systems had been offering service, connecting Russia to France and other countries.

Connections in Paris seemed the best chance of reaching Germany.

The Russians purchased his ticket to Paris and awarded him with some rubles to convert in Paris, which helped him complete his trip to Germany.

Borden was lucky. It was evident that most captured soldiers would never make it home.

He believed God wanted him to come home to his family and surviving friends. He would forever be thankful to God, having survived this terrible war.

His family listened carefully to his every word, with tears in their eyes.

The Berger family had miraculously survived this long and vicious world war that had taken its toll on most of the globe.

CHAPTER
TWENTY-EIGHT

Hermann and Anna's wedding was to take place in the welcoming room of the Dortmund Hospital.

Management offered to supply the food for a luncheon.

Hermann's mother Ima made a white dress for Anna from material donated by the laundry.

Dr. Hermann purchased a new officer's uniform from the local military supply building that had been rebuilt. His uniform could not have any emblems on it per the new regulations.

A cake was being made special by the kitchen for the joyous occasion.

Ida rearranged Anna's beautiful hair.

Borden, Hermann's father, obtained a bottle of good German wine that had somehow made it through the war.

And little Luz Berger would be old enough to see his mother and father get married.

Fifteen nurses and volunteers would be present at the ceremony.

Father Otto Shultz, a Lutheran Minister, would perform the ceremony.

The wedding was set for Friday at eleven o'clock.

Come Thursday, everyone was busy finishing up the final touches.

Anna began praying for the memory of her brother Ivan and her mother and father whom she believed were murdered by the Nazis.

She asked God to give their souls to Heaven where they would enjoy an eternity of peace.

Hermann, always an optimist, suggested to Anna that the records of their passing just might be available through the government records that had survived the war.

He encouraged her to attempt to check the availability of the records when she could find the time to do so. Hermann volunteered to help her in the quest.

Friday was about to arrive. Everything appeared ready.

CHAPTER TWENTY-NINE

Father Otto Shultz was late. He had fallen, tripping over some bricks in the street.

He arrived at the hospital with a bandage on his knee and a bruise on his right hand. Nevertheless, he was prepared to conduct the wedding ceremony.

Dr. Hermann Berger was ready to marry his sweetheart, Anna Kanopsky.

The room was packed with individuals. There was to be no music as music was not yet readily available to the survivors of the war.

And so, Borden Berger was to give his new daughter-in-law away, so to speak.

Hermann stepped forward to take her hand and led her to their position in front of the pastor.

Ima and Ida stood by.

The ceremony took just about ten minutes, and then they were formally pronounced man and wife. Hermann kissed the bride.

The crowd clapped their hands and shouted in German, "Good luck."

The proud father, Borden, broke open the bottle of wine and passed it to the newlyweds.

After tasting the vino, they passed it around to the audience. It didn't quite make it to the end of the group, but no one complained.

Borden and Ima made an announcement. "We give to you Hermann, Anna, and Luz, the deed to our property that was demolished during the war.

We want you to build yourselves a home on that site where Hermann and Ida were born, and where we all lived for so many years."

"Please, accept this gift. We will attempt to help you rebuild, when it becomes possible. Don't worry about Ida, Ima and myself as we have already put our names on the list to soon live in the new public housing, already being built, in downtown Dortmund.

We are excited about the move and are looking forward to a new life in this new building, probably with many friends that have survived, as we have."

Hermann quickly responded, "Your gift is beyond wonderful. We cannot capture the words of thankfulness we are feeling for your generosity. Luz is sure to enjoy the location, like Ida and I did, growing up at that site. Anna and I will begin to draft a home to be constructed there as soon as it becomes possible."

Hermann reached across to help wipe the tears coming from Anna's eyes.

The wedding cake and luncheon followed, catered by the hospital kitchen staff.

Father Otto stayed for the meal and celebration. Borden gave the pastor a few marks for his kind service performance.

Although they had consummated their marriage long before this ceremony, the newlyweds left the group after the luncheon, and once again continued their obvious love affair in a room on the second floor.

The wedding day ended with smiles and laughter.

Weeks later, they announced that Anna was once again pregnant.

CHAPTER THIRTY

It was nine months later to the day when Anna (Kanopsky) Berger gave birth for the second time.

This time, it was a healthy baby girl whom they named Beatrice, after her late mother Beatrice Kanopsky, who Anna was certain had been eliminated by the Nazis during the war.

Baby Beatrice now joined Luz in the Hermann and Anna Berger family.

Hermann's parents, Borden and Ima, had just moved into their new apartment in the public housing building in downtown Dortmund.

Plans for the rebuilding of a house on their former site had been completed nearly two months earlier.

With a grant from the United States Marshall Plan, Hermann was able to get the money to begin building the planned structure.

Other money also became available from the Dortmund Hospital and from a new stipend that was received from the German government by Borden for the work he had completed for the German government, during the war.

The Dortmund Hospital also donated six chairs and lent them two beds, mattresses, and linen until they could purchase their own items.

An advanced military survivor check began arriving at the first of each month for Dr. Hermann Berger.

Hermann believed that he could now afford new furniture.

Luz was now walking and talking like an adult at only three years old.

His sister Bea was crawling and mimicking Luz with great clarity.

The family was two weeks away from moving into their new home. The finishing touches were being applied to the interior workmanship.

Anna had planned a special party for the family to be held on the second day of occupancy.

Hermann purchased local food and drinks for all. It was to be an important achievement in their new lives, and celebration was clearly appropriate.

They even invited the pastor, Father Otto, who quickly accepted the invitation.

The house was finally completed, and the happy family moved in on the same day.

As promised, the celebration party would take place on the very next day.

And that next day had finally arrived.

CHAPTER THIRTY-ONE

The party in the new house was terrific.

Everyone was happy, enjoying good food, drinks and merriment.

Their children had already taken over the house, and toys and games were scattered everywhere.

Even Father Otto had a good time.

Spoiling the celebration was a letter that arrived requesting Dr. Hermann and his sister Ida attend an investigation regarding the war.

The meeting was scheduled the next week in Nuremberg, on Monday at noon.

The letter didn't reveal the purpose of the investigation, but Hermann thought that since they asked for Ida to be present, it probably meant it had something to do with her hiding Anna during the war.

"We will have to wait to see what this is all about," he stated.

They continued celebrating, to the best of their ability, the completion of the new house built on the grounds where the Berger family had lived for nearly thirty years.

Borden and Ima were full of joy for their son, daughter-in-law, and their two grandchildren.

This family had endured the war with all its negativity and outcome. They had faced danger at every turn and still managed to hold onto the faith and courage needed to make it through the terrible incidents that their country's leadership had brought upon them.

Now they felt that they had turned the corner and had finally been able to take steps toward the rebuilding of their lives.

Each member thanked God for their survival, noting that more than one third of Germany did not survive. Hermann had asked his family and guests to take a minute, to quietly thank God for his mercy and deliverance.

The party ended on an upbeat, with smiles, hugs, and handshakes.

CHAPTER THIRTY-TWO

Monday, the day of the interrogation, had arrived.

Dr. Hermann and his sister made their way to Nuremberg, Germany. It took several trains for them to make it to their destination.

Just before noon they were able to locate the building that was to house their meeting.

An open room on the third floor was where they were to meet their interrogators.

The brick building itself was half destroyed during the war, yet the other half was still being used for administrative work.

Three military officials were there to meet them. They asked Hermann and Ida to please sit down.

"I am Major Blandford of the British intelligence. This is Simon Markoff of the United States legal bureau, and this is Craig Pearlmenstein, former Wehrmacht officer attached to the Nazi SS."

They had been attempting to find German individuals who might have played death roles in the war, especially those regarding women and children, and Polish victims as well.

We have investigated a Gestapo agent named Claus Smidt who last was working in Berlin with the deportation of Jews to concentration camps. He claims that before, he had been working in Dortmund, arranging young Polish and Jewish women to spend weekends with worthy German officers.

Smidt mentioned a lost girl, by the name of Anna Kanopsky who had been assigned to a Dr. Hermann Berger. He also mentioned that he thought you Hermann, might be hiding her somewhere in Dortmund. He even spoke of investigating his sister Ida who had been working as a nurse at the Dortmund Hospital.

"What do you make of Officer Smidt's memory?" he stopped speaking and waited for Hermann to reply.

"I know that during war, many things change, and I had found the young woman assigned to me to be very intelligent, kind and beautiful. We actually fell in love. I am now married to her, and we have two children. I could not let her go back to the bus, having heard that these women were to be eliminated," Dr. Hermann stated.

"Yes, this is exactly what we are investigating. We believe that he Officer Smidt was responsible for some twelve busloads of young women who were eventually taken out to the countryside, shot, and buried there throughout a good portion of the war."

"Other German officers say that they do not believe such an atrocity could have happened, but we have found the remains of their bodies and are in need of someone like you to help us bring this man to trial and receive the appropriate punishment. Your story is quite believable. We would like to know how you were able to save Anna Kanopsky," he completed.

Hermann was quick to respond, "Both Ida and I were against the destruction of Jews. We thought that they were being wrongly accused of all the problems created by our country's leadership. On that basis, we decided to help the Jews, whenever possible. When I was assigned Anna, I was expecting a Jew, not a Pole. And little did I know, we were to fall in love from the very start of that weekend. My sister devised a plan for Anna's escape and it worked well. Anna was hidden in Ida's room at the hospital for the remaining days of the war. As you may know, I lost my arm in an explosion while serving the country as a medical doctor in Bremen. I am very lucky to have survived. I would be honored to help in your attempt of bringing Officer Smidt to trial."

"Excellent. We will contact you once again, anticipating a trial date here in Nuremberg quite soon. Thank you two for attending this meeting and we look forward hopefully to the trial so we may bring to justice the killers responsible for eliminating so many people during this terrible war."

Hermann and Ida returned to Dortmund.

They agreed that the potential trial was important, indeed.

CHAPTER THIRTY-THREE

Borden Berger had his back examined by a new physician who started his practice in downtown Dortmund.

The doctor carefully pulled out the remaining shrapnel that had found its way into his back during the war. Other body areas had healed with time.

He finally felt quite good and thought he could consider a job possibility if he was able to procure one that suited him.

Ida began scouring the newspapers that had risen in the community.

She spotted an ad in which a company was looking for a reliable individual who could manage a rebuilt travel agency.

Borden had not traveled beyond Germany since before the beginning of the war.

Previously, he had visited France, the Netherlands, Spain, and England.

He had always been desirous of traveling to Switzerland, Ireland, Scotland, Wales, Belgium, Poland, and Hungry.

"I will apply for the position. Maybe I will get my chance to finally visit some of these countries!" he exclaimed.

Ida thought he could handle the job and the challenge.

Sure enough, Borden Berger was hired to manage the New Germany Travel Bureau located just a few blocks from their apartment building.

The rest of the Berger family was delighted for him.

Borden was first being sent to Hamburg for three days of training.

His salary, which was already more than fair, would be supplemented by sales commissions.

Ida had been hired by the Dortmund hospital as an experienced nurse. She was thrilled for the recognition and the actual job position.

She would now have income for herself. The five years as a volunteer had given her the background to serve well as an official nurse.

Her mother became a nurse volunteer at the hospital as her daughter had been during the war.

Anna was thrilled to be a mother to Luz and Bea but wanted to take on some part time work to make her life more meaningful.

Her ability to speak and write fluent Polish attracted several rebuilding organizations.

She was finally hired by Volkswagen at the beginning of a marketing program they hoped would help sell their newly adjusted military vehicle to other countries.

Anna was to help communicate with Poland, who was still rebuilding, following their own devastation from the war.

Her part time position included work completed from her home, allowing her to remain active in the lives of her two growing children.

Hermann, because of his missing right arm, had job limitations that would keep him from permanent employment. The new local government, however, became interested in him, hoping he would consider leading a voting committee that would begin a more formal government for the City of Dortmund.

Not only did Hermann take the job, but he decided that if this opportunity went well, he might stay in politics and continue serving the area.

The Berger family had found new hope in Dort-mund, Germany.

All of Germany had begun to arise from the ashes of defeat, carrying with them a new vision of hope.

CHAPTER
THIRTY-FOUR

Dr. Hermann Berger received a second letter. The investigating committee into war deaths had decided on a trial date. It was to be in three weeks.

He and Ida were to report to the Palace of Justice in Nuremberg at 1 p.m. on Wednesday of that week.

They were to be prepared to represent the prosecution against one Gestapo agent Claus Smidt.

Major Blandford of British Intelligence would be their contact.

Hermann and Ida began going over their knowledge of Claus Smidt, and particularly, any information they had learned about the methods the Nazis had been using when the two of them were brought into the picture.

Finally, the day of the trial arrived. They once again took trains to Nuremberg.

A military vehicle met them at the train station to take them directly to the Palace of Justice.

The Palace of Justice was the site selected by the International Military Tribunal, upon the end of the war in 1946, where post-war trials on twenty four of the most important political and military leaders of the Third Reich had taken place, under the Control Council Law No.10 established by the Allies, back in 1943. (Many of the criminals committed suicide, and most of the rest were hanged.)

The Allies and their representatives unanimously agreed to a "Declaration on other German atrocities in occupied Europe."

They also agreed to pursue the leaders of these other German atrocities, "to the utmost ends of the earth."

The trial of Gestapo agent Smidt appeared to be one of these other leaders.

Hermann and Ida met up with Major Brandford of British Intelligence.

The major was prepared to inform them of their approach in hopes of a quick conviction.

He wanted to assure them of the role they had been asked to play in the trial itself.

Hermann was dressed in his new German basic uniform without emblems of any sort.

He would be addressed as Captain Doctor Hermann Berger.

Ida was also going to be called upon as his sister and savior of the assigned woman who would eventually become her brother's wife and her sister-in-law.

The trial was set to begin at 2 p.m.

Defense lawyers numbered three. The prosecutors presented two lawyers and seven witnesses. There was a jury of seven military representatives from four Allied countries. The Judge was Malcomb Northgate, a lawyer from Scotland. Acting clerk and English interpreter was Seymour Liggette, from France.

The trial began and finally, Gestapo agent Claus Smidt was brought into the trial room handcuffed.

Clerk Seymour Liggette announced the arrival of the judge and everyone in the court room stood to welcome him.

Judge Northgate took his seat and immediately banged his gavel.

"Please take your seats," he shouted. "This trial will now begin."

CHAPTER THIRTY-FIVE

L ittle Luz Berger, walking and talking, began bossing his younger sister around the house.

Anna thought the kids were doing just fine.

She began her work at Volkswagen, sending letters to potential Polish customers directed by their marketing people.

Her handwriting was excellent, but she started taking typing lessons from an assistant director at the Volkswagen plant.

The job called for her to work three days a week from 9 a.m. to 1 p.m. Anna loved the challenge, and it still allowed her plenty of time to spend with her children.

Her mother-in-law, Ima, who only volunteered at the hospital in the afternoon, was available to mind Luz and Bea on the mornings that Anna worked at Volkswagen.

The arrangement was working quite well.

Even Aunt Ida, when she was available, would find the time to come and play with her nephew and niece whom she absolutely adored.

Borden would arrive, often without notice, to spend precious time with his grandchildren.

Hermann would play with them whenever time permitted, enjoying the role of fatherhood.

Hermann and Anna's love for each other was always visual and romantic.

Yes, the Berger household arrangements were excellent considering what they had been forced to endure during the war.

They were a family, and they would never forget the insecurity and danger they
had faced during those terrible years.

Their obligation to God, for their survival, was apparent.

CHAPTER
THIRTY-SIX

The clerk presented the case against Gestapo agent Claus Smidt.

"Upon an investigation performed by three members of the Allied Military Committee, it was discovered that this man, Gestapo agent Claus Smidt, was instituting a program dictated by the Fuhrer's Official Office to offer selected young women captured during their campaign to many of the officers of the Third Reich for weekends, as a favor.

Further, the accused took it upon himself to gather up these mistreated and abused women after their forced weekends and bring them to the country-side where he directed four of his assigned soldiers to systematically kill some twelve buses-full of these women, throughout the war years, and to bury them in graves atop the spot of their elimination.

Further, Agent Smidt, upon hearing that the war was ending, personally brought his four soldiers who were instructed to kill the women to the same countryside, where the accused, using his own revolver, shot and attempted to kill all four soldiers. What he did not know, though, was that one of the soldiers did not die and has lived to tell the whole story. He is here, among others, who will confirm this horrific happening to the jury, for a hopeful quick sentencing."

The judge replied immediately. "Let us now hear the defense's statements, please."

Lawyer Yosep Gritz responded, "My client pleads not guilty. He was, and still is of the belief that Berlin wanted him to eliminate any and all associated persons utilizing harsh treatments before the end of the war. I am here to plead for his life on this statement alone."

Rebuttal Lawyer, Sidney Friends questioned, "Then why did he eliminate the women throughout the war?"

Lawyer Gritz answered, "The original plan was dictated by Herr Fuhrer Himmler in formal documents that have since been destroyed. In that capacity he was only following orders, those he was forced to perform. Please take this fact into consideration."

Rebuttal Lawyer Friends responded, "We have asked committee leader Major Blandford of British Intelligence to present the first of our witnesses. Major Blandford, please."

Major Blandford stood and immediately began, "I have before me a witness to the program for selected German officers that had been arranged by the Nazi's headquarters. The witness had been given a woman, for a weekend, whereby he was encouraged to enjoy sex and other favors. His personal experience was quite different, as he will tell us. Please, welcome Captain Doctor Hermann Berger."

Hermann rose from his chair and walked slowly to the podium.

"I grew up in Dortmund, Germany where my next store neighbor was of the Jewish faith. He was a special man of great wisdom and knowledge. We went to school together. He was one of my best friends.

My father worked with two Jewish men in a small business owned by a fine Jewish family.

When the Nazis began blaming all their troubles on the Jews, everyone in my family was appalled.

To make matters worse, they came and took them all away.

They also took over the business my father worked in and sent the owners to the concentration camps for extermination.

We were so upset that my sister and I decided to attempt to save anyone who might be in suspected danger from that day on.

I was entering my second year of medical school when I was forced into the Wehrmacht as a Doctor of Medicine, without a degree, and without any bodily training or experience.

They sent me for limited training, with others, and eventually to the university campus at Dortmund where the officer-women program was about to start.

My sister had heard about the program and its performance in Berlin and so she knew of the results for the women involved.

So, when the program began in the Dortmund college campus, she and I knew about the final solutions that would be instituted.

My sister, Ida, developed a plan for my assigned woman's escape.

She is here to tell you personally of her successful plan of escape, and how she saved this young woman's life.

First, I must tell you that we did not know that this girl was going to be Polish Catholic instead of a

Jew, as had been expected. Regardless, our only motive was to save anyone we could.

Also, I did not plan on falling in love with her, or her falling for me. This did indeed happen, however, and it made the planned escape even more important for me, and to my sister, as well.

My final piece of information to you is that Anna Kanopsky, the escapee, and I have been very happily married and have two children in our family today." Hermann finished and sat down next to his sister.

Major Blandford stood up and spoke, "I want the Jury to know that we approached several officers who had experienced those weekends, and no one would believe that these women were killed soon after spending time with them. Only Captain Doctor Hermann Berger would agree to be here today. We are very grateful for his genuine rendition of what took place. Now, I would like to continue hearing of the successful escape plan put forward by the Doctor's sister, Ida Berger. Please welcome her."

Ida Berger received a pat on her back from her brother and rose to approach the rostrum.

She began, "I am Ida Berger, sister of Dr. Hermann Berger. When I was told by Hermann that he was about to receive an assigned woman, I knew that we should, at least, attempt to save her. I devised such a plan for the attempt.

Hermann and I met secretly on the first morning outside his temporary living quarters on the campus of Dortmund College.

I told Hermann of my proposed plan. He thought it might work and asked to attempt it on the second night of the weekend.

Waiting until the second night was not my idea. Hermann requested it, as he needed the extra time with the woman. I did not argue with him.

And so, on the second night of the weekend, the plan would be attempted.

We knew that if we were not successful, we would all pay dearly, possibly with our lives.

The plan centered around my old and used bicycle which I had ridden to his campus location on the morning of our first meeting.

At twelve midnight, the campus guards, all being Nazis soldiers at this time, would be changing positions.

Also, many of the workers at the college would be ending their shifts and would be heading home at that time.

I thought that their movements would offer us the best timing for an attempted escape from the campus area.

Roughly two miles away was the Dortmund Hospital where I was working as a volunteer nurse.

I was given a room in the rear extension of the hospital on the second floor with other volunteers and nurses.

As my room was private, I believed I could easily hide an escapee.

The young woman, Anna, was to leave Hermann's room at 11:45 p.m., and not a moment before.

She was to ride my hidden bike through the campus entrance and meet up with me.

The bike would be abandoned, and she and I would walk the remaining mile and a half to the back door of the Dortmund Hospital.

I was prepared to keep her in my room until the war ended or, at least for as long as possible.

The plan worked quite well, and I was able to protect her in my room for the duration of the war.

When the war ended, my brother Hermann returned though without his right arm.

Today, I am proud of what we accomplished, having saved one woman from the horrific death that was scheduled for her.

She is a wonderful woman, wife, mother, and sister-in-law.

My family is blessed to have survived the war and we have begun living a new life full of gratitude and peace.

Thank you for the opportunity to tell my story."

Ida returned to her seat and hugged her brother.

The British Major immediately began introducing his next witness.

"Please welcome Colonel Neiss of the French Armament Battalion who was the leader of the investigation committee that had been formed to trace death programs other than those connected to the concentration camps.

Colonel Neiss spoke, "We came upon the burial locations at the countryside of Berlin and at Dortmund. We were able to identify many hundreds of women's remains in shallow burial areas at both locations. As you will hear from a surviving guard, our investigation confirms his statements on what actually took place at these two sites. All the women's bodies clearly showed bullet holes into the body cavities randomly."

Colonel Neiss returned to his seat.

The Judge called for an hour recess.

CHAPTER
THIRTY-SEVEN

The recess was over. The Judge banged his gavel.

"Please present your next witness," he shouted.

Major Blandford called "Heinrich Weisel."

Mr. Weisel rose from the rear of the courtroom and walked briskly to the podium.

In broken English he remarked, "I am Heinrich Weisel. I had been put in charge of the movement of the selected women being investigated today. My family was all bakers and I was being groomed to be one as well when I was forced into the Wehrmacht, like so many of us were, just prior to the start of the war. I had received a memo from Berlin, explicitly stating that these women were to be treated with reverence, and that they required the upmost care in their delivery to the Dortmund college campus. When I heard what had happened to these young women, I was shaken in disbelief. I did not want to do anything for the military after that news had reached me.

Of course, I had to continue to do other things asked of me. I had no choice but to continue serving the country. It has bothered me ever since, and I am ashamed of having taken part of such horrors, no matter how small my part was. I pray that there will be peace once again here in Germany, and that someday the world will find a way to forgive us for what we did."

He slowly worked his way back to his seat.

The British major introduced his next witness.

"My name is Boris Hesse. I was the only one of four soldiers that survived Gestapo Officer Smidt's final killings.

When I was fifteen, I was inducted into the Hitler Youth Program whereby I was indoctrinated into full Nazi thinking and prepared to serve our Fuhrer. I was completely brainwashed to the extent that I would give my life for him and only him. When I reached eighteen years of age, they assigned me to Gestapo agent Claus Smidt. I joined three other soldiers and we were sent to a firing range for extra training. When we returned to Smidt, he immediately ordered us to prepare for military action. We did not know what kind of action would be required.

Upon encountering the first group of women subjected to the weekend program, we were told that these women had cheated on our country, infested our officers, and were Jews of the worst order who needed to be eliminated at once. We were ordered to kill them and kill them we did. It didn't end there, though.

At least a dozen more times we were commanded to repeat this action, and when the war was coming to an end, he brought us back to the countryside where we had killed so many. And there he shot the four of us. He emptied his Luger into each of us.

I was fortunate. His first shot hit my back, to the right of my spinal cord. The second one braised the side of my head, causing bleeding. Smartly, I had fallen to the ground and pretended to be dead.

He finished off the final soldier and left the scene.

I was able to stand and walk to the road where, within an hour, I was picked up by a farmer and given medical attention.

I stayed with the farmer for nearly four weeks, until the war finally ended. The farmer and his family will always remain my special friends.

As a survivor of the war, I am very thankful to have been as fortunate as I was. I seek forgiveness for what I did. Please, I have remorse for what I did. But understand the conditions were not of my making. I will never fire a weapon again.

Please, God, forgive me."

He returned to his chair.

The judge once again banged his gavel and announced, "I've seen enough. Let us go directly to the defense summary, please."

Lawyer, Yosep Gritz returned to the stand and spoke.

"As all your witnesses have related, they were ordered to do their jobs. But Gestapo agent Claus Smidt was ordered, also. His commands came directly from Berlin, just like those of your witnesses. He too would like God's forgiveness. The accused admits his guilt and should be treated, as most Germans having been forced to serve their country and the military, with mercy.

Hitler and his administration may deserve the worst, but not their soldiers. I rest my case."

The judge banged his gavel. "I request the jury go and decide on this case as quickly as is possible. Court dismissed until called once again."

CHAPTER THIRTY-EIGHT

The jury entered the courtroom, and everyone stood once again.

Bang went the gavel, "Please be seated."

Judge Malcolm Northgate asked, "has the jury reached a verdict?"

A female French air force officer rose from her seat, "yes, we have done so, judge."

Judge Northgate returned, "please read to us your final verdict and explanation."

The young French officer began her findings, "I am Rosalie Cervette, senior pilot from the now destroyed Mercury Legion Air Force Terminal near Calais, France. Our terminal was completely blown up in one Nazi air encounter. During that event my brother, Pierre, was killed. My father was captured by the SS and tortured to death. My mother was exterminated in the Dachau concentration camp. Henri, my fiancée, was shot and killed near Paris. My sister is still missing, and I don't have much hope for her survival.

I came through the war as part of the French Underground. I am lucky to be here and to be the chosen leader of the jury.

It should also be noted that the other members of this jury have lost close to fifty loved ones. They too, would have much to say if given the chance.

However, we, as a group, have considered this terrible case without personal prejudice, and I must say that has been quite difficult, for which this case that has come before us. We have also taken into consideration the German people.

Our decision is based upon general logic and indicates the charges that must be made. The world has and will be forever watching the results of this terrible war, and we must not ignore the obvious wrong doings by mankind.

On that basis, we have recommended to the court the following steps, agreed to by all members of this jury.

Heinrich Weisel, transportation driver, two years of community work.

Boris Hesse, the only survivor of four German soldiers who had killed hundreds of women under command of Gestapo agent Claus Smidt, sentenced to five years in a French prison.

Gestapo agent Claus Smidt, who led the murdering of hundreds of women and personally shot four of his trained killers, is hereby sentenced to life in a British prison.

May there never be a need, like this one, to be tried again. The world deserves a better future. God bless the lives of all survivors of this horrific past."

The young French officer returned to her seat in the jury box.

Judge Northgate followed up with, "By the power that has been given me, I hereby accept the Jury's findings and require the appropriate military actions to enforce these verdicts. This court is now adjourned."

He gave his gavel a resounding bang for the last time.

Hermann and Ida left behind their personal feelings for the verdicts but were anxious to leave the courtroom and make their way home.

On the train, Hermann said to Ida, "They were too lenient. Claus Smidt deserved to be hanged, and the young soldier should have received twenty years in prison."

Ida responded, "We can never punish all who committed crimes, but one or two more helps the

Allies, and the good German people find some reprisal in the trial. I'm just glad it is over."

Finally, the train stopped, and they were once again returned home to Dortmund.

The following afternoon, when Ida had returned from the hospital, she picked up the Dortmund Daily Scribe newspaper waiting at the doorstep.

Its headline read: GESTAPO SMIDT SUICIDE.

Yes, Gestapo agent Claus Smidt had taken a cyanide capsule on his way to his life sentence in Britain.

He was pronounced dead at the scene.

Prison authorities from London had taken him aboard a train when he somehow reached into his pocket and swallowed the capsule.

Military investigators believed he was given the poison by an outsider.

Smidt had joined the list of ongoing cheaters who lacked the courage and decency to face the penalties that mankind had justly placed upon them.

Of course, that list began with their proud, godly Fuhrer who denied Europe and the world redemption.

CHAPTER THIRTY-NINE

As most know, Germany was beaten to the ground by Allied Forces.

They had demolished their key factories, airports, railroads, bridges, military installations of all kinds, and in the process killed a great number of their population.

The survivors began clearing rubble, damaged war vehicles, and bodies from the streets.

A great process of rebuilding was to take place.

Many known Nazi co-conspirators were put to work clearing roads and highways.

Because they had lost huge numbers of their men, women were forced to partake in the rebuilding as well.

The Allies agreed that their primary concern now would be to keep out Communism.

If Europe could recover together, they would have a better chance of stopping the Communist effort around the globe.

The United States Congress approved the Marshall Plan, named after our war hero, General George Marshall, whereby they gave Europe many billions of dollars to reconstruct.

Most of the money came to Germany, some to Britain, and some to other countries as well.

Families like the Berger's reunited and pieced together what little was salvageable from the destruction.

Dr. Hermann Berger was to live to age seventy-seven.

He had become a prominent citizen of Dortmund, and soon became the mayor of the city.

Five years later, he became a leader in the German Parliament, newly organized in the city of Bonn.

He never again practiced medicine and enjoyed his life with family.

Anna (Kanopsky) Berger became a popular home economist, mother to two great children, and always thrilled to be the wife of her first and only love, Hermann.

She kept her association with Volkswagen/Poland and even visited there for a conference.

While there, she visited her own family location which had been totally destroyed. But finding the Catholic Church half standing, she went inside and made a prayer in memory of her family members.

Borden Berger, Hermann and Ida's father, died of a stroke, at age 64.

His wife Ima lived another seven years and passed away at age 71.

Luz Berger, son of Hermann and Anna, lived to be a world class soccer player and became quite wealthy.

He was to marry a British tennis queen, Angela Bruce. They were to have three daughters, Minnie Berger, Mynie Berger and Morene Berger, named equivalent to *Minny, Mynie and Mo.*

Beatrice Berger, daughter of Hermann and Anna, became an airline stewardess, traveling the world. She met an American pilot, Captain John Sweeney, and the two were married. They are still traveling around the globe – somewhere.

CHAPTER FORTY

When Hermann became Mayor of Dortmund, he was able to access files meticulously kept by the Nazis of those processed and eliminated during the war.

He found no mention of Anna's brother Ivan but found the name of their mother added to a list of those exterminated at Dachau.

Hermann once again encouraged Anna to attempt to locate him, saying "He may have survived. Who knows? You have nothing to lose by trying other methods."

Anna wrote to the Polish International newspaper for recommendations on how to pursue the possibility of finding her brother.

They offered back-checking of their three years of publication since the end of the war. No information was to materialize from it.

They did, though, offer a free ad continuing to help finding lost family members.

Anna wrote an ad asking for anyone knowing the name Ivan Kanopsky to please respond to the newspaper directly.

They were to run the ad for three weeks.

Brother Ivan, who was living in America with his wife Brenda, believed that his mother and sister had both been eliminated by the Nazis.

While in the concentration camp, a guard had told him that, "your mother was to be eliminated and your sister, if she was pretty, might be saved for the officers... and then killed."

Based on that statement, Ivan was to believe that there was no hope for survival for either of them.

His wife, Brenda, herself of Polish decent, had continued to view the Polish International news-paper when it would arrive each month. One afternoon she came upon his sister's ad.

She screamed for Ivan to come and read the insert.

It was now nearly three years after the end of the war and reasonable communications had been returned to most of Europe.

It afforded Ivan, and his long-lost sister Anna, the opportunity to have many conversations via telephone to piece together their own experiences, and to recount their early life in Poland.

She told him of her children Luz and Beatrice, named after their dear mother and father.

Ivan cried onto the telephone receiver and had to wipe it dry.

Anna invited Ivan and Brenda to visit her and her new husband Dr. Hermann Berger in Germany.

Ivan quickly refused.

He made it clear that he could not return to Germany – the country that destroyed his parents and life in Poland – and that it would be very difficult for him to accept her husband who was a member of the German military, even in his limited role.

"Maybe you could change my mind later, but for now, I am not in a receptive mood regarding Germany or its people.

Also, I cannot and will not buy any products coming from Germany even though their products are mostly well-made.

I hope you understand.

My love for you remains a priority.

I only trust that Hermann will treat you well and that you get to enjoy life that you deserve.

It has been my long-time wish that my sister, somehow, would survive, and you have done it.

God's hand surely must have guided you through it all.

May God continue to bless you, my God given special sister."

ABOUT THE AUTHOR

 A life-long Rhode Islander, Burt was raised in Providence and Pawtucket in a family with a diverse musical presence that inspired him to pursue the piano, trumpet, baritone horn and vocals, and develop a profound love for jazz.

The former owner of several successful businesses throughout New England, Burt is now retired and lives in Cranston, Rhode Island.

Burt is also the author of *'Round Newport: Recalling 60 years of Jazz Around Newport, RI, Discovering Newport, Breakfast with Jackie O and Other Stories, Treated as a Jew,* and *Capmaker for the Czar: An Immigrant's Story*